GINGHAM DOG
P R E S S

Columbus, Ohio

HUSH!

A FANTASY IN VERSE

DOMINIC CATALANO

To my daughter, Sara, who taught me to listen
And in loving memory of my mother, Virginia Mae Mayer

Children's Publishing

This edition published in the United States of America in 2003 by
Gingham Dog Press,
an imprint of McGraw-Hill Children's Publishing,
a Division of The McGraw-Hill Companies
8787 Orion Place
Columbus, Ohio 43240-4027

www.MHkids.com

Library of Congress Cataloging-in-Publication Data is on file with the publisher.

Printed in the United States.

1-57768-679-9

1 2 3 4 5 6 7 8 9 10 PHXBK 09 08 07 06 05 04 03

The McGraw-Hill Companies

Hush little darling, don't say a word,

Daddy's gonna give you a . . .

mockingbird.

If that mockingbird flies away,

Daddy's gonna take you to the park to play.

If it rains and cold winds blow,

Daddy's gonna take you to a movie show.

If that movie makes you frown,

Daddy's gonna take you to a play downtown.

If the lead should lose her voice,

Daddy's gonna give you his best Rolls-Royce.

If the car should sputter and die,

Daddy's gonna take you up high in the sky.

If in flight your head starts to whirl,

Daddy's gonna take you around the world.

If the cruise is too slow paced,

Daddy's gonna take you into outer space.

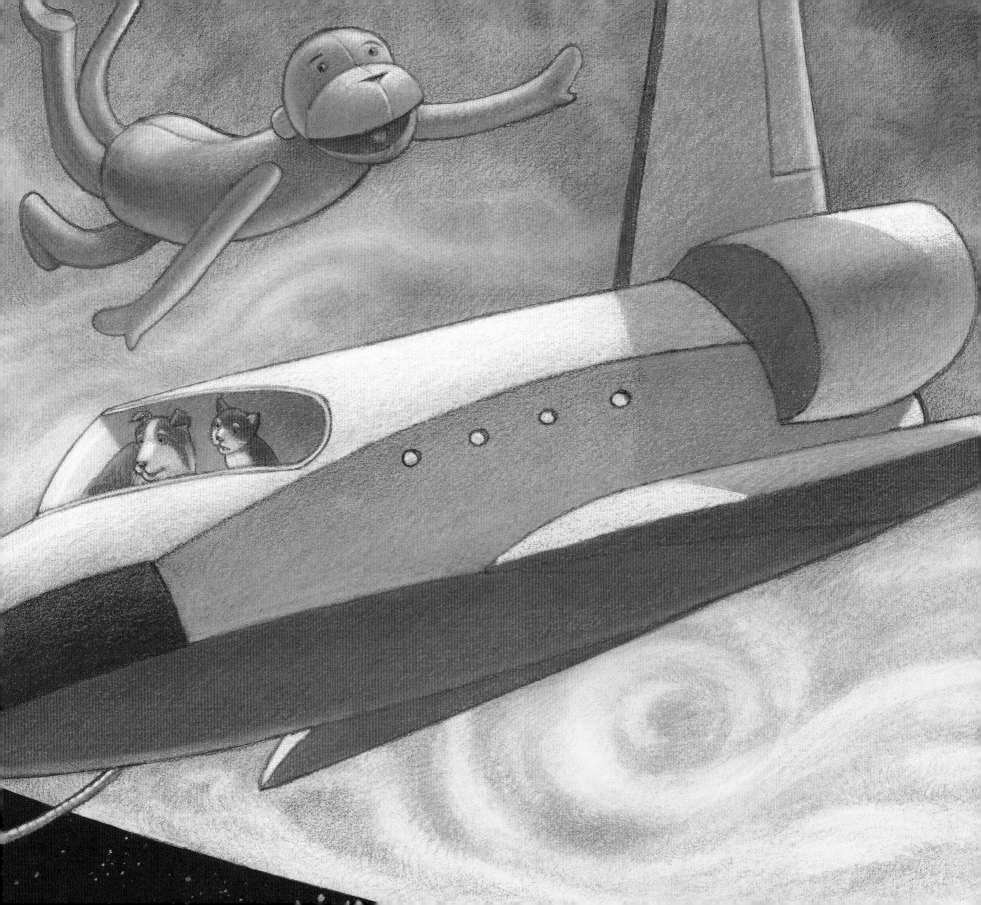

If your daddy plays a clown,

You'll still be the sweetest little darling in town!